STORIES FROM THE WORLD OF ETHEREAL

A Short Story Collection

RAYMOND S FLEX

CONTENTS

DISHWASTER

BRIGHT YELLOW LIGHT bled into the side alley to Hempy's Happy Times, a fast-food restaurant with a long and distinguished history in the town of North Bruxley. A man-boy: the frame and muscular build of a man in his early-twenties, but the cherubic face of a youthful adolescent, stumbled out into the alley, turning his ankle in a pothole as he fell, catching his head on a brick sticking out at a malicious angle from the wall.

A stern and heavy voice, surely belonging to a stocky man in his forties or fifties, followed the boy out. "That's the last dish you smash in my kitchen, you bleeding dishwaster."

The door slammed shut, extinguishing any light in the side alley.

The boy sat on the ground, rubbing his head where it had come into contact with the wall.

There was a girlish titter in the darkness.

The boy flinched then glanced round. "Who's there?"

Another titter.

"What's so funny?"

A match scraped against an unseen matchbox and flared up, sending a flaming glow round the alley—

showing up the various wheelie bins, the broken glass sparkling in little circles of chaos and the bones chewed up by stray dogs. All the smells seemed to join soon after. The sweet smell of rubbish juice and rotting meat.

The flame steadied and girl brought the match up to her face, illuminating her features. She had dark brown—no, black—eyes and china doll features, as if were someone to tweak her nose it might break, if they were to touch her rouge lips they might crumble into dust. Her black hair was in a pixie-like cut and it shimmered with every one of her movements.

The boy straightened and then rose. He looked back to the door which he had been recently hurled out of. He swore under his breath.

"What's the matter?" the girl said.

He looked back at her. "What're you doing here, lurking about?"

The girl shrugged. "Just bored, I reckon."

"Yeah? So thought you'd pop down here, look out for any pot washers getting sacked? Thought it might be worth a chuckle?"

"Your boss said it was a dish."

The boy wiped his nose with the back of his sleeve. "I do dishes, too."

She arched an eyebrow. "You really are a jack-of-all-trades."

"Why don't you go pick on someone else, eh?"

Her grin widened and she stepped closer. The match burnt down to her fingers and then snuffed out, leaving them in fresh darkness.

The moon draped its half-light down on the side alley. After a matter of moments the boy's eyes grew accustomed to the change and he could make out the form of the girl.

"Have you got a girlfriend?" the girl said.

The boy scowled. "What kind of a question is that?"

The girl shrugged. "Dunno, just curious."

The boy sighed. "Look, you turn up here just after I've lost my third job in as many months, first you laugh at me getting thrown out on my arse then you start probing into my private life. Are you some kind of self-esteem murderer?"

The girl tittered again. "All right, dishwaster, don't get your knickers in a twist."

"Don't call me that."

"Why not?" she said. "It's funny."

"That's my career you're making fun of."

She flicked her fringe out of her eyes. "Then maybe you should consider another one."

Dishwaster shook his head and snorted. "Yeah? Great advice, I should really take that on board. Only problem is there's something standing in my way, namely qualifications."

"What's that?"

Dishwaster screwed up his eyes. He made his way along the alley, wanting to pass the girl. "Get out of my, way, please. I want to go home. There's some lichen cultivating on the seal of my fridge that might be missing me."

The girl shoved her hand against Dishwaster's solar plexus. "Come on, you haven't listened to what I've got to say yet. Stay and natter, just a little while."

He waited a moment and then knocked her hand away, making for the main road, heading back to the bus stop to catch the Ebberly Express back home. As he trudged his way along the pavement, he noticed the *pitter-patter* of footsteps behind him. When he turned his head, sure enough, there was the girl, following.

He came to a halt, leaning up against a convenient lamppost, plastered with dishevelled posters advertising gigs, flats for rent and lost dogs. Since his t-shirt was caked in baking fat and grease he really didn't care about the extra layer of dirt he was adding to the fabric. "All right," Dishwaster said. "That's enough of this. Stop following me, all right?"

The girl trod up to him. She smiled. "No."

Dishwaster looked round, as if he might be able

to spot a passing policeman, bring the law to bear on this. "You know, what you're doing is tantamount to stalking."

"'Tantamount?'" she said. "That's an awfully big word for a dishwaster."

"I told you not to call me that."

Ignoring him, she closed one eye and looked him up and down. "I think there's more to you than meets the eye, you know. I reckon you're doing yourself down."

He patted the pocket of his jeans and withdrew a battered packet of cigarettes. Inside one cigarette remained. It was bent in the middle so he straightened it out before slipping it between his lips. "Great, so now you're feeling bad about making me feel bad."

"Smoking will kill you."

"Yeah? Thanks for the lecture, Grandma, now give me a light, won't you?"

The girl's inane smile dialled up a couple of notches. "I don't have a light."

"Look, don't get all high and mighty with me, okay? I saw that match you struck back there in the alley, now hand one over."

"That was the last one," she said.

"You really want to enrage a nicotine addict?"

"I'm telling the truth."

Dishwaster gazed into her eyes, those dual pits of

oil and murk, and he decided that she was telling the truth, or at least she was a passable liar. Apart from that, though, he had to admit she was attractive, that he was attracted to her. It made him all the more frustrated when the pretty girls were nice to him—like dangling something he could never have before his eyes.

He spat out his cigarette and smushed it with the heel of one of his raggedy trainers. He marched back off in the direction of the bus stop.

"Where're you going in such a hurry?" the girl said.

"None of your business."

Dishwaster kept up his pace, hoping the girl would get bored and wander off. She was one of those kooky types who either completely understood their sexiness and used it to mock innocent boys or she was genuinely unaware of how good-looking she was, and was some kind of mental.

He reached the bus stop and took a seat on the wooden bench. The planks creaked beneath his bottom, threatening to crack right open. It would be just his luck for that to happen.

Still not having taken the hint, the girl walked into his vision once more. A smile continued to part her lips, adding a glow to her cheeks.

"What do you want?" Dishwaster said, a growl bubbling in his throat.

The girl stood before him, looking down, the same pert features and oblivious expression. "I don't have anywhere to go."

Dishwaster stared at a particularly interesting puddle of crap in the road, hoping the girl would get the idea and scarper. But she remained there, still not getting the hint. Finally, he sighed and looked up at her. "Do you want me to suggest some places you can go or what?"

"Okay," she said, with the same carefree tone of voice.

Dishwaster pressed his hand to his clammy forehead, still smelling the stench of the third-rate detergent his boss demanded he use on the job. Although he had been wearing rubber gloves the scent had still got through somehow.

He brought his hand back down and counted off on his fingers. "You can go: to Atlantis, El Dorado or Hell, take your pick."

She scowled at him. "I've already been to those places. I don't think there's much point in me going back." She brightened. "But I could take you there with me if you like."

Great, a joker, thought Dishwaster and leant forward

in his seat to look round the girl, to check that the bus wasn't sneaking up on them silently. Unfortunately it wasn't. He pressed his shoulder blades back against the hard wooden planks and stared up at the cloudy sky.

"Can I come home with you?" she said.

The question caught Dishwaster on the chin, like a left-hook in a darkened club, just after three in the morning, after several bouts of mixed drinks, and maybe some recreational drugs too. He got out just about the appropriate response to reflect that sentiment. "Wha?"

She jiggled her shoulders, as if a chill had crept up on her, then said, "I want to come to your house, can I?"

The bus appeared at the top of the street, its green neon lettering piercing the gloom: Ebberly Express.

Dishwaster stepped out onto the curb, waved his arm at the bus. He glanced back at her. "You got your own transport card?" he said.

Seemingly out of nowhere, she produced the distinctive yellow card and waggled it in front of his eyes.

He looked up and down the street, wondering whether this might be some kind of setup. But, then again, who would bother to set him up? He was such a champion loser that some random stranger had taken it upon herself to christen him Dishwaster.

The bus creaked to a halt, a cacophony of hydraulics accompanied by a *guff* of exhaust.

"Come on, then," he said, as he stepped onto the bus and flashed his transport card at the scanner.

The scanner beeped them both on board.

2

D ISHWASTER'S FLAT was pretty much as he left it. There was a half-eaten pizza on the crooked, circular kitchen table, still wallowing in its own greasy cardboard box. A little further along, the single bed remained unmade, its duvet scrunched up on the floor. The bathroom at the other end of the flat smelled much the same as before.

He glanced over to check out the girl's reaction to the scene.

It seemed that she was an especially good liar because she kept up her inane smile as she walked through the deeply-set filth and decay. When she reached the fridge she opened the door and inspected the grey seal around the edge. "Hello there, lichen."

Now he was sure she was a nutter, and he regretted bringing her here, back to his place. How would he manage to get her out the door without that weighing on his conscience? He felt responsible for whatever might happen to someone as vulnerable as her.

She slapped the fridge door closed and turned on him. "I take it you don't have a girlfriend, then?"

"You have terrific skills of deduction."

"Thanks," she said, with a little leap in her step.

And a faulty sarcasm detector, he thought.

As he watched on, the girl helped herself to a tour of his flat. The way that she peered at things, reached out to touch them, even smelled a couple, reminded him of a dog inspecting an unfamiliar home, working out where it fit in.

Once she ducked back out of the bathroom, apparently finished with her solitary tour, she looked over at him. "I never told you my name, did I?"

"No," Dishwaster said, already anticipating that he was going to regret hearing it—what was it they said about pets being much more difficult to get rid of once you named them?

"It's Pixibob."

That just about figures, he thought.

"Aren't you going to ask me about it?"

Whatever attraction he'd felt toward her before seemed to dissipate with his exhaustion. He really had no patience for any more kookiness. He wasn't one of those guys who slaved after girls, a while ago he had resolved that he was perfectly happy alone, wallowing in his miserable flat, doing his miserable job. Generally being miserable.

He stretched his arms so that his fingertips brushed the lumpy ceiling. When he yawned, his mouth seemed to latch open wide enough to eat a small baby. "To be honest," he said, "I'm completely knackered. I've just put in an eight-hour shift scrub-bing pans, I'm ready to go to bed."

"That's all right," she said. "We can sleep."

At this remark his ears perked up some more. His tongue felt thick and unwieldy in his mouth. Was his imagination playing tricks on him or was she indeed throwing herself at him? What else could that mean? He had to get things straight. "There's only one bed," he said.

"I know," Pixibob said. "We'll fit, won't we? I'm only little."

He couldn't argue with that.

He thought about her, surely an extremely vulner-able person, and he hated to think what might've happened to her if she had come across some other, more oafish, pot washer. To tell the truth, he might've been more oafish if he'd had a modicum of energy.

"Uh," he said, scratching the back of his neck.

Pixibob launched herself forward and leapt onto the bed, the springs creaking a couple of times as she landed. She rested her head back on the pillow, shut her eyes and immediately started to snore.

Dishwaster watched on, puzzled. He had never seen anyone go to sleep that fast, it was like she could do it on demand or something. However, his eyes drooping in their sockets, he got in beside her, pulled the duvet over both of them and clicked off the light.

In the morning there was no sign of Pixibob, and Dishwaster considered whether it had all been a dream. He drew the duvet down to his chest, seeing that he was still fully-clothed. Perhaps it had all just been a dream—one weird, warped dream.

Once he'd had a bowl of cereal and knocked back half a mug of cold coffee, which he'd found on the kitchen counter from the day before, he ventured out of his flat, glancing up the corridor before stepping out as if Pixibob might be waiting to pounce at a moment's notice.

Seeing the coast was clear, he slunk out along the corridor then out of the building. There was only way to see if yesterday had all really been a dream. He would have to go back to Hempy's Happy Times and see if he had been sacked. That would shine a light on all this.

When he arrived his boss was strutting his way behind the counter, dishing out orders to the servers as they saw to the morning line of customers, four or five long. It was enough for Dishwaster to make eye contact with his boss to cause a kerfuffle.

His boss's eyes bulged from their sockets and his complexion darkened. "What in hell's name are you doing here, layabout?"

"Uh, uh," Dishwaster got out, backing up toward the doors, seeing his opportunity to rush for freedom.

The boss rounded the counter, his belly jiggling over the waistband of his trousers. "Out, go on, get out of my restaurant."

Some of the customers turned their heads in Dishwaster's direction, but before he could cause any further commotion he was out, into the car park, jogging away from Hempy's. About a hundred metres later he was out of breath, sweat dampening just about every part of his body. He doubled over, resting his hands on his kneecaps, and took a moment to catch his breath. When he snapped back upright, Pixibob was staring right back at him.

3

"HELLO!" she said.

Dishwaster winced, took a step back. "What . . . where, where did you come from?"

"I don't know, really."

"Last night, you disappeared."

"Oh," she said, touching her index finger to her lower lip, "I let myself out. I had some things to do."

Dishwaster got the feeling that this conversation would only proceed in circles if he were to ask what 'things' she'd had to do. "I . . . I thought you were imaginary." He scoffed. "I thought that yesterday was just a dream, that I wasn't really fired after all."

"Nope," she said, with relish. "Everything really did happen yesterday."

He flashed his eyebrows. "Well, thanks for your sympathy."

"Oh, stop moping about feeling sorry for yourself. I've got a proposal for you."

He began to walk his way along the pavement, toward a corner shop where he could buy a newspaper and get a head-start on the 'Help Wanted' section. If he was lucky he might not even need to give the details of his last job—make a clean break, start anew.

Pixibob kept up with his pace, skipping her way along beside him. "You're just going to keep making the same mistakes over and over again at this rate."

He stopped dead, faced up to her. "Listen, you, you've got no idea who I am, what my life's about, so I don't need any of your stupid proposals, all right? I live in the real world. There's rent that needs paying." He ducked his head to his armpit and sniffed. "Didn't even get a shower this morning because I'm trying to use as little water as possible. So why don't you just bugger off?"

Pixibob's smile faltered and then, against all odds, she started to cry. She breathed heavy sobs, her hands pressed against her eyes. Her shoulders trembled slightly.

Dishwaster glanced up and down the street, worried that someone might be watching on—have seen the situation and believe him to be some kind of aggressor. He stooped forward, laid his hand on her shoulder. "I'm sorry, I didn't mean to be that direct. It's . . . it's just that you don't want to get involved with a hopeless case like me." He managed a smirk. "People like me are better off alone with their negativity, their lack of hope."

She broke off her sobs a second, looked out through her fingers, eyes wet with tears. "That's just what I've been trying to tell you, Dishwaster. You aren't hopeless. You've got all the hope in the worlds."

He wondered whether he should pick her up on her choice of the word 'worlds,' but decided that it was better to just let the delusional be: live and let live, or scrub and let scrub as he had coined in his pot washers' union of one.

He stared at his shoes, the scuffed toes and thought about how much of a failure he was. He recalled being back at school looking at a kid call Walter Johnson, fat and stupid, worse than him at everything: PE, maths, English, you name it. But, just the other day, he'd seen him zoom past in a fairly-new, compact city car . . . wearing a suit. No, there was no doubt that there was something wrong with Dish-waster, something irreparably wrong.

"So, you want to know what I've got in mind or what?" she said, a glint in her eye.

He looked at her, then up the road, where the corner shop awaited—all those pot washing opportu-nities. He analysed the rest of his day stretched out before him, he would arrive home, strip down to his boxers and call up all the adverts. After that, assuming he didn't get an offer for tonight, he would veg out in front of the TV: daytime talk shows, auction programmes and, a little later, kids' cartoons.

And then he thought about Pixibob—this beautiful girl who had, somehow, taken a shine to him, wanted to offer him something. What did he have to lose? So he lolled his head to face her and said, "Go on then, what's this great offer you've got for me?"

Pixibob's freckles danced across her cheeks like rogue atoms. She beamed at him, exposing her perfectly-straight, perfectly-white teeth. She reached out and snatched hold of his wrist, her grip firm and sure—much stronger than anything he would've had a prayer at wrenching off.

She dragged him past the corner shop with the newspapers glaring back at him through the windows, and then they proceeded through a park. After the park, they entered and then left a busy shopping centre, Pixibob dodging in and out of the shoppers. When they approached a graveyard, marked: Rutsley Church and Burial Grounds, Dishwaster said, "Where're we going?"

"Shh," Pixibob said, looking round, her eyes rolling in their sockets, as if someone might be listening in.

Without giving Dishwaster another chance to protest, they slipped through the gates of the grave-yard and made their way up the gravel pathway, leading up to the church.

A tremor ran up his spine. He should've seen this coming. "Look," he said. "If you think you're converting me, going to yank me into that place and splash some holy water on my head then you've got another thing coming. I'm not—"

For the first time during their acquaintance, Pixi-bob's patience wavered. "Would you please shut up?"

Taken aback by this sudden change in tone, Dish-waster did.

4

THEY PROCEEDED along the path—to Dishwaster's relief—away from the church, going round back. She brought them to a stop beside a plaque emblazoned onto one of the buttresses. It was made of slate and had once been black, but now it had a green tinge to it. Before Dishwaster got the chance to read the lettering, Pixibob snatched hold of his hand in hers and pressed them both up against the plaque then she mumbled something in a strange language.

Nothing happened for a few seconds and then, all of a sudden, the colours in the world round them bled into one another. A blinding white filled Dishwaster's vision and he felt himself being whisked away on an invisible pair of beating wings. He lifted up off the ground and screamed. He screamed his head sore and when he caught he breath he started to scream again.

A shudder passed from Pixibob's hand into him and only when they came to a stop did he realise that she was laughing her head off at him, laughter lines webbing their way round her eyes. She wiped away a stray tear, rolling down her cheek and sucked in a deep breath, trying to compose herself. "What's the matter?" she said. "You never broken through all time and matter?"

Now he was beginning to suspect that she had slipped him something. He had no idea how she'd done it but he was certain. Back there, on the road, when she'd seized hold of his hand. Might she have injected him with something? If he were high on something then he would have no way of knowing. "What did you say?"

"Time and matter. You've broken through. We just shot through a portal, left your world behind. That plaque, that was the key. Just have to touch it and say the magic words."

"Obviously," Dishwaster said, feeling faint.

She released his hand.

Dishwaster examined the pitted marks that her fingers had left behind on his hand and thought, already, about how much he craved her touch again. It had been a long time since he had touched a girl— been skin-to-skin with one who wasn't his mother or sister. But he cast his sensitive reflections aside while he looked round.

They were still in the graveyard, that was for certain, but it was night. The day had passed them by and now the moon shod its light upon them. The moon, it had changed from its cheesy-yellow, the yellow of the fungus which grew between his toes, to a light purple. The light it gave off was purple. A kind of twilight glow.

When he tried to look beyond the tilted grave-stones, beyond the crooked wall of the graveyard, it all grew blurry, similar to the effect of a heat haze. He turned round and looked off over his shoulder. A gasp caught in his throat. Gravestones spotted the land-scape for as far as he could see. Hills rose up out of the land, forming into snow-capped mountains in the distance, still the rutted forms of the gravestones appeared. He looked back at Pixibob.

She reached out, rested her fingers beneath his chin and, lightly, closed his wide-open mouth. "No flies round here to get caught in there, but you're better off not looking totally gormless for your placing."

"My . . . my, what?"

"Come on," she said, seizing hold of his wrist and yanking him onward.

As they went on their way, he noted the soggy ground beneath his feet. With each step his foot would sink into the earth. It felt mulchy and untrust-worthy, like it might give at any time. He suppressed this immediate concern, trusting that Pixibob knew what she was doing here in this world as much as she didn't in his.

They weaved in and out of gravestones, some at

impossibly obtuse angles, seemingly ready to pop from the earth at any second, and then Dishwaster caught his train of thought and managed to get the words out. "Where are we?"

Pixibob waved her hand vaguely at the landscape around them, dotted with gravestones. "This is the End of Time."

"Erm, the End of what?"

"Time. This is the end of the world, the only part of the Earth which survives in any form whatsoever. Every human ever to live on the face of the Earth has a monument here. It's a bit like the index of all humanity." She wrenched him forward. "Get a move on, will you? We might be outside all reference to time and space but that doesn't mean you can drag your heels."

Who would've thought Rutsley Church and Burial Grounds would be the last location in all time and space, he pondered.

They approached a small building formed of grey bricks. There was a bell to the side of the doorway with a notice which was scrawled in toddler-like handwriting: Rin fur Atenshun.

As they passed by it, Dishwaster said, "Maybe this place is right for me after all. Even I can get my grammar right with something like that."

Pixibob became serious. "Don't make fun. If you

had to keep a catalogue of every person who ever existed in this graveyard you might not have enough time to think about *grammar*." She depressed the buzzer.

An ominous clanging, like a dampened church bell, *donged* from somewhere within the structure.

"You said we were on a different world," Dishwaster said.

"That's right, this is a different world. Doesn't look much like yours, does it?"

"Well, yeah, no, but the point is that we're all stored here? I thought there would be a bunch of other worlds, you know, with different creatures and stuff." He paused. "Like you."

She grinned. "Oh, don't you worry about that. There are. Lots more. But let's take things slowly, shall we? Little baby steps is the key to getting your head round things."

A midget appeared in the doorway. He, or she, had a mop of tangled, white hair which brushed at his, or her, shoulders. When he, or she, opened his, or her, mouth to speak he, or she, cleared a large wad of phlegm from . . . its throat. "Blooming heck, Pixibob, you brought in another one, so soon?"

Dishwaster felt a little offended that there had been others.

"That's right," she said, then turned to Dishwaster. "This is Divus."

Trying to keep his voice low so as not to offend the midget, Dishwaster said, "Is it a 'he' or a 'she?'"

"A 'he,'" she said, with a glowing smile.

Divus stepped to one side and allowed them inside, his eyes crawling all over Dishwaster as he slipped by.

Another midget was stooped over a log-burning stove. It looked up at them as they passed by.

"Don't mind us," Pixibob said, then, bringing her lips close to Dishwaster's ear, said, "That's Doris. She's the female end of this partnership."

"You mean there are only two of them, looking after the entire history of humankind?"

Pixibob gave him a side on glance. "Don't flatter yourself, dear, you're really not as important as you think you are."

They arrived in an arched hallway. Pixibob led them up to a wooden door, rapped twice and then opened up, bringing Dishwaster in behind her.

A large man with a beak-like nose and bird-like, marble eyes, watched them in. He shuffled some papers off to one side and interlocked his fingers. "This the new one, Pix?"

"Yup, all ready to go. Should've seen him back in his own time, eking out a living washing pots."

"And dishes," Dishwaster said.

The large man harrumphed, as if Dishwaster had spoken out of turn, then he plucked up a thick tome with a crumbling leather cover. Pieces dropped from it like flaked skin as he handled it. He flipped through the pages, reaching the middle of the book and then said, "There is an opening, down at the river, in the Ethereal world. Year 42, 730, 914."

'Ethereal,' that sounds nice, thought Dishwaster.

"Your name's Dishwaster, eh?" the large man said.

"Actually it's—"

The man held up his hand. "It really doesn't matter. From now on you shall be known as Dishwaster, or would you prefer *'The* Dishwaster?'"

Not really certain how to respond, Dishwaster said, "Just Dishwaster's fine."

The large man met Dishwaster's eye then, with a flick of the pen, marked something in the book. When he'd finished, he said, "All right, Pix, take him away."

"Cheers, Frank," she said.

5

A S PIXIBOB turned Dishwaster away from the man at the desk, twirled him out the door, back through the graveyard, questions throbbed through Dishwaster's brain—he wanted to know what was going on, where he was being sent and, finally, what he would be required to do.

However, before he had the chance, they passed through a creaky wooden gate and into another expansive graveyard where Pixibob forced him to touch a gravestone. Soon enough they were spinning through the air, smashing through time and worlds, or something, before they arrived at what Dishwaster supposed to be their destination. Ethereal it was. It matched its name precisely.

Beneath his feet, he examined the lush green grass, the trees in leaf and, a little further along, a stream burbling its way beneath a stone bridge. To one side there was a cottage built out of—what seemed to be—mud, stone and twigs. A chimney smoked grey smoke. All in all everything looked very homey indeed.

Pixibob led Dishwaster by the hand to the door of the cottage and brought him inside. There was no lock on the door. The interior featured a sturdy wooden table and an open fireplace, the flames licking at the flue. In the corner of the cottage was a bed, well-made, and clean-looking.

Dishwaster wondered how often the cleaner came by to look after the place.

Pixibob trotted up to the bed and peeled back the cover, looking down on the mattress. "It's stuffed with goose feathers, you know."

"Oh, great," Dishwaster said.

Pixibob frowned. "You aren't allergic, are you?"

"No, no, nothing like that. It's just that, you know, all this. I mean, is this all for me. Really?"

"Yes."

He took stock of the situation, thought of anything important he might've left behind in his dishevelled flat back in his own world. His TV and laptop were probably the most valuable items, but there didn't seem to be any power outlets here and, most likely, no Wi-Fi.

"Urm," Dishwaster said. "What do I have to do here?"

"Do?" she said.

"Yeah, like a job. What's my job here?"

Pixibob jabbed her finger up in the air. "Ah, glad you asked." She stomped across the room, over to a cabinet. She opened it wide to reveal stacks and stacks of plates within. They were all gleaming—the cleaner here must've been very good indeed. She stood back from the cabinet. "There," she said.

He approached the cabinet, looked over the plates, then glanced back at her. "Uh, I'm not quite sure I've made the leap here. What am I supposed to do with these?"

"Isn't it obvious?"

Worried that he was pre-empting what he most feared, that he had been brought here to wash plates, or dishes, he held back. "No," he said.

Pixibob eyed him up and down, then slid a plate out from the cabinet. Since she took one from somewhere in the middle of a pile, it looked like all the plates were about to fall to the floor in one giant landslide of crockery. However, somehow, mysteriously, the plates remained in order, a slight wobble the only noticeable effect.

She clutched hold of Dishwaster's hand, dragged him out the cottage and up to the path which lay beside the stream. She crouched down low, plate clutched in her hands. "It's very simple, really. All you have to do is wait here for a hero."

He thought about asking what she meant by 'hero,' but he supposed that being here, in this fantastical place, he really should've put the pieces together for himself. So he got down beside her, feeling the

warmth of her breath on his skin, it sending shim-
mers along his body hair.

They seemed to wait there for hours, in the same
position, the truth be told Dishwaster lost track of all
time altogether, glad to be there beside Pixibob,
catching her face in profile, absorbing her sweet,
peachy scent in his nostrils.

And then, just as it seemed they would remain in
stasis forever, there was movement on the horizon, a
figure coming over the hill. As he descended toward
them, his hair long and blond, clutching a wooden
shield and a shining, golden sword, Pixibob leant
back on her heels, brought the plate back behind her
head and, with all her strength—considering her
grunt which would've rivalled even the most
committed female tennis player—she lugged the
plate at the hero.

The hero swaggered onward, unaware of the
projectile frisbeeing toward him. He only caught
sight of it at the last moment as it struck him on the
forehead. He crumpled to the ground, his sword
clanging down beside him and his shield landing with
a wooden *thunk*. Pieces of broken crockery lay sprin-
kled around him.

Dishwaster glanced toward Pixibob. "Is . . . is
he dead?"

"Nah," she said. "You just slowed him down."

Dishwaster observed the knocked-out hero. "Won't he be angry when he comes round?"

"Oh, definitely. But he's got a quest to accomplish, and you're just a minor obstacle, so I wouldn't worry too much about it. He didn't see either of us. All you've got to do is hide away in your cottage and wait for him to go away."

"And that's it?" Dishwaster said.

She grinned at him. "Yup, told you this'd be more satisfying than washing pots and pans, didn't I?"

"Won't it get, you know, a little repetitive?"

"No more than washing pots. That's why I chose you. You're suited to doing the same thing over and over again without asking too many questions."

Dishwaster considered this statement, wondered whether it was an accurate, if blunt, statement of his character. Examining all the facts, thinking over what he'd done with his life so far it was difficult for him to deny.

"Anyway," Pixibob said, "it's not like you've got much choice. I doubt you'll be able to work out how to get back to your world."

"Probably right."

She rested her hand on his shoulder and led him back toward the cottage.

As they got closer to the door, Dishwaster worked up the courage to ask the question which had been bothering him ever since his arrival to Ethereal. "Erm, are you going to, like, going to stay here with me."

Pixibob turned full-on to him, peeled her hand off his shoulder and then, flashing a grin, said, "Nope," and promptly disappeared in a puff of smoke.

Dishwaster stared into the air, watching the last of the smoke evaporate and wondered what on Earth —or was it Ethereal?—he had got himself into. He looked back to the hero, whose limbs now twitched a little, his head rising from the ground, and beat a retreat for his cottage. And, as he tugged the door closed behind him, feeling snug and safe in his new home, he managed a long and satisfying smile, the first for quite a while.

BALD POET

I

SYDNEY, otherwise known as Bald Poet, because of his distinctive, shiny bald head, sat slouched against the corridor wall, his feet stretched out before him, and emitted a long and unchecked sigh. As he contemplated suicide—for the thirteenth time that day—a court aide tottered out into the hallway. He had large, bulbous eyes and a scrawny frame. His shirt looked too large for him, flapping over his waistline, while his trousers—tights really—clung to his legs, the latest fashion. A fashion which Sydney had no intention of being swept up in.

The aide puffed out his cheeks. "Bald Poet, the King wishes to see you."

"Does he now?" Sydney said, staring at his booted feet, wondering how long it would take for his toes to fall off if he ceased to move them.

"Yes. You must come quickly, he really is in a foul mood."

"Oh dear."

The aide lingered there, blinking far too often and swinging his arms by his sides.

Sydney lolled his head upward to make eye contact with the aide. "And what makes you think that poetry shall cheer him up?"

"We've tried everything, music, players—we even had a sword fight take place right before his chair, one of the men was badly injured but the King only stifled a yawn."

Last resort as usual, Sydney thought. He had no intention of going into the court, last time the King had threatened to roast him alive, testicles first. There were bad crowds and then there was King Fredrick. "That *is* a predicament and a half," Sydney said.

The aide swung his arms some more, clearly wanting them to get a move on, lest he get in trouble with the King.

Sydney sat there for another few seconds, contemplating whether or not he should get up, appease his master or—should he say—*attempt* to appease him. Then, looking at the young aide, he realised that the poor boy might be put to the death if he failed to bring the Bald Poet to the court. King Fredrick had been putting an awful lot of people to the death recently.

Feeling his bones creak and groan in protest, Sydney wrenched himself up into a standing position.

A smile appeared on the aide's face. He skittered from side to side, as if being blown about by a light breeze. He writhed his hands together and looked to Sydney expectantly.

"Let's go see him, then," Sydney said, feeling heaviness overwhelm his heart.

2

THE COURTIERS were clearly on edge. Everyone was standing for a start, and that was never a good sign. The window which occupied the entire wall behind the throne revealed the grey skies outside. The clouds formed molten lumps, while rain pelted down. It all seemed quite ominous.

King Fredrick, himself, perched on the edge of his throne, lips stuck in a pout with his head resting on his leaning arm. When he looked up to see Sydney approaching, he rolled his eyes, grunted and muttered something about 'bloody poetry,' under his breath.

Sydney, keeping his smile pinned on, and his mind alert to any pointy ends which might find themselves directed toward him, approached the throne, gave a bow then the hint of a grin. "If it might please Your Grace."

Fredrick glanced off to the side, to his senior, portly aide, Jenson. "Hasn't it stopped raining yet?"

"No, Your Highness."

Fredrick flared his nostrils then returned his attention to Sydney. "Go on then, what've you got for me."

Sydney's smile was already starting to strain the

corners of his mouth. All this pretence really got to him—he knew he never should've jumped at the chance to get paid for his art. He cursed the day a royal talent scout had taken him aside, from his crate in the middle of a town square, and handed him a contract. He would get some serious frowning done this afternoon, provided he still had his head by then.

"What would you like to hear, Your Grace?"

"What've you got?"

"Well, I have epic poems, a quiver full of sonnets, perhaps a ballad?"

"Any limericks?"

Sydney's heart sank a little further. "Ah, yes, I have some limericks."

"Give us one, then."

Sydney thought of his room, his books stuffing the shelves, all those that he'd acquired over the years he'd been here, since he'd been making a living, had the money to obtain more and more. But what did they mean when he had no chance to stretch his professional wings, when his patron had no concept of poetry, that he wished only to hear . . . limericks.

Jenson sneered at Sydney. "Come on then, be quick about it, eh? We'll bring in the jester if you can't manage to have us crack a smile."

The jester, Sydney thought, *always that damn, alco-*

holic, deadbeat jester. What really peeved Sydney was that Jenson knew exactly how to get to him. He rolled his shoulders, locked his fingers together and held his hands at his waist, then began:

> There once was a lady from Faylee,
> Who thought she could lay thee,
> But, she was distraught,
> When by another king she was bought,
> And never felt she the pleasure of
>   thy willy

Fredrick remained stone-faced.

A cruel smile of satisfaction took hold of Jenson's face.

Sydney had trialled that limerick several times in his bedchamber, thought about whether or not he would ever have the nerve to deliver it in front of the King, and now he had he regretted it more than anything else in his life. It was like he had come before the King, begging him to stick his head on a pike.

And then a marvellous thing happened. The King's mouth curled round the edges and then he slapped his thigh. He barked laughter and, after a reverential second's pause, the courtiers joined him in laughter.

One by one, Sydney's muscles relaxed.

Fredrick chuckled away for a fair few minutes more before he held up his hands and called the court to a hush. He fixed his eyes on Sydney and said, "You have cleared my head this bleak and rainy afternoon, and I thank you for that, Bald Poet."

Sydney had never liked that name, but it had stuck to him ever since Jenson had registered him as part of the castle. All the same, he did his best to smile and look unperturbed by the King's sudden swing in affection for him.

Fredrick rose from his throne, strode over to the window and looked out. "It seems that the clouds are clearing after all." He glanced back over his shoulders. "Sometimes I wonder whether the gods smile prouder on their mortal ruler when he is in a good mood."

Jenson licked his lips. "Yes, Your Highness, I'm sure they do."

Fredrick looked over to Jenson, parted his lips as if to speak, and then turned back toward Sydney. He gave him a warm smile. "I wonder. This evening Lord Runtleston is planning to visit. His father, the duke, has sent him here to make some kind of deal, and I've been puzzling over the evening's entertainment all day. Dear Bald Poet, would you do us the honour of performing for us tonight?"

Truth be told Sydney had hoped that, following the fairly successful delivery of his limerick, he might be granted the opportunity to fade into the shadows of the castle for a little while. But now, with this fresh performance tonight it only meant another chance for Fredrick to get Sydney's head on the chopping block, especially considering he had such a distinguished guest. Despite taking all that into account there really was only one response he could make and hope to keep his head till this evening.

Sydney glanced over Jenson and received a scowl for his trouble. He bowed his head to the King. "My Lord, I would be truly honoured to perform for you this evening."

"Good," Fredrick said, slumping back down on his throne with a grunt.

One of his many maidens approached him. She had shapely breasts and buttermilk skin. She wore a crimson robe which barely reached her thighs. She took up a seat on the arm of the throne and fed Fredrick grapes, popping each into his mouth.

Slightly distracted by the maiden, Sydney missed Fredrick's next remark. "Beg your pardon, Your Highness?"

Fredrick gave Sydney a steely glare. "You'd better not disappoint me this evening, Bald Poet, or I'll have your head on a pike overlooking the drawbridge before morning."

At least I know where I stand, thought Sydney, and promptly excused himself from the court. He scuttled off through the castle back up to his bedchamber.

3

A S SYDNEY arrived back in his room, the sun streamed through the clouds, entered through his narrow crack of a window. He dropped into his leather-bound chair and stared at the dust rising through the air before him, like golden flakes. He considered scribbling down his observation, but, in the end, decided it to be nothing at all that would interest a king.

Of course he had tomes and tomes of poetry he'd written over the years, but this occasion called for a bespoke work. He had to write something involving the King, and his distinguished guest, what had been his name . . . Lord Runtleston, that was it. He fished out a rogue roll of parchment from between two volumes, flattened it with the palm of his hand, dipped his quill in a pot of black ink then scribbled away.

He reached the conclusion of his work around the time that one of the members of the house brought him up a plate for dinner. He had been just about to slip down to the service quarters, to dine with the rest of the servants. Never had dinner been brought up to his bedchamber. As he forked his way through his pork and potatoes, he considered whether this was his king taking special care of him or some kind of Last Supper. He supposed that he would find out very soon.

He snatched up the roll of parchment and skipped down the stone staircases, worked his way through the spiralling corridors, until he reached the banquet hall. As etiquette demanded he waited at the door until Jenson waved him inside.

Fredrick sat chewing on a leg of beef, pieces getting stuck in his beard as he went.

His guest, Lord Runtleston, sat nearby. He had brown hair and a wispy beard. He couldn't have been much older than twenty. A pair of women from the King's own brothel—or 'maidens,' like the one from the afternoon, as they were euphemistically termed—sat either side of him, feeling up his fledgling muscles, and cooing at his 'rugged' skin.

The atmosphere seemed somewhat frosty. Neither the Lord or the King made the effort to converse with one another. Perhaps it had something to do with the difference between their ages. Sydney speculated that King Fredrick was affronted that Runtleston had deigned to send his son in his place—although not uncommon, Fredrick, having a king-sized ego, like most kings, had obviously taken it as a personal insult.

And so, now everything fell to Sydney. It was his

responsibility to rectify the evening.

King Fredrick caught a glance of Sydney and visibly brightened. He set his leg of beef down into his bowl of broth, plodded over and slapped him on the back. He addressed the hall with his arm round Sydney's shoulder. From the state of the King's breath, Sydney was sure Fredrick had flushed home a cask or two of wine.

"This man!" Fredrick said, a couple of decibels too loudly. "He has the prettiest wit in my whole kingdom. This afternoon he tickled me with limerick when I was feeling down in the mouth and he comes to us tonight, Lord Runtleston."

Runtleston looked away from his prostitutes . . . maidens, with a slight daze in his eyes. Obviously this was one of his first visits away from his father's side, and he was somewhat overwhelmed by the superstar status afforded by his title.

Fredrick continued, "He's agreed to indulge us a while with his poetry." He released Sydney, took up his place at the head of the table, where a maiden immediately took up beside him, mopping his beard clean of beef pieces. He waved his hand at Sydney. "Go on then, Bald Poet, give us a few verses."

Sydney unrolled his parchment and cleared his throat. He glanced round the room, to see everyone steeped in silence, all of them focussed on him, wanting to see whether or not the King's judgement had been accurate, because if there was one thing a king specialised in it was the art of the overstate-ment. His eyes found his first line and he read:

> A lord hath come to the castle,
> See how he rides his noble steed with
> > dignity and grace,
> Hear all that now a lord hath come to
> > the castle.

Sydney glanced up to get an idea of the receptive-ness of his audience. All still concentrated on him, the King more than most, his forehead rippled with wrinkles. He continued:

> He hath come to see our king, our
> > noble king,
> Who hath waited so long to meet with
> > the Lord,
> And whence will they dance? Who
> > shall say?

At the end of this verse there were several blank looks round the hall. Sydney's throat tightened and his pulse throbbed in his ears. He'd better get on with it, get out of here as quickly as possible.

And tonight they shall celebrate,
> together,
Within their own embrace,
The night shall be gay and full
> of merry.

King Fredrick held up his hand. "Pray, Bald Poet, what is the point you are trying to make with this verse?"

Jenson stepped out of the shadows. "My Lord, I do believe that he was insinuating that you and the Lord shall have, erm, conjugal relations this night."

A shudder ran up Sydney's spine. Thinking about it, the lines he had written, he had failed to check for any double meaning. It had been written in a hurry and he'd had no time to study it for such intricacies. "Oh, no, Your Highness, please, if you would allow me to continue, perhaps it shall become obvious, what the poem is trying to say."

The parchment slipped through his fingers, fluttered to the floor where it got sodden in a puddle of beer or wine, or piss.

Sydney stooped, recaptured the parchment and looked to Fredrick. "Please, Your Highness, allow me to continue, I promise that all shall be resolved."

Fredrick elbowed his maiden aside, prompting her to skitter away, back to the harem. He crossed his arms over his chest and looked on with expectation.

Sydney took this as his opportunity to continue.

> In the morning they shall go their
> separate ways,
> The King to his throne, the Lord to his
> father,
> And shall speak ever more of their
> encounter.

A lump formed in Sydney's throat. He dared not look over the top of the parchment. It was bad, it had sounded really bad, and now, he was sure that he would pay for it with his life.

Jenson lurched forward, spoke in the King's ear, so that no one else heard his words. Much to Sydney's disgust, the King nodded along with whatever it was that Jenson said, no doubt he was being sure to put the nails into Sydney's coffin, one by one—if he was to be lucky enough to have a coffin at all.

King Fredrick nodded along then gestured for Jenson to leave his side. He got to his feet and stared across the banquet table—strewn with food scraps and overturned cups of wine. "For this gross insult to the King's honour you shall be taken down to the dungeons where you will be kept indefinitely."

Although Sydney felt terrified of his fate, he thanked the gods that he had not been put to death —not yet anyway. He told himself that he could've done no more, that, whatever poem he would have read tonight, he would've met with the same fate.

A pair of guards tweaked his arms behind his back and chained his wrists together. As they led him away, Sydney took in the banquet hall, the King, who had already turned back to the table, actively glowering into the remainder of his food—clearly stuck right back in his foul mood. When they reached the doorway, Sydney managed to get a look over at Jenson, who smirked back at him, glad that he'd completed his task, taken down another entertainer. Sydney speculated whether Jenson might not be the main reason for the King's eternal melancholy, with an advisor so keen to point out the faults in the world, large and small.

But now wasn't the time to protest, that would only be risking his neck. No, Sydney would have to do his time in the dungeons, no doubt stay down there until after the King had had Jenson fired, or executed, and subsequently forgotten the reason why Sydney had been sent down there in the first place. Sydney was determined to survive, if only to spite Jenson.

THE GROTESQUE

1

JOHN STONEFIELD played with the other children, darting in and out of the alleyways, skipping along the crooked cobblestones and screaming his head off. It was a market day and so the streets were packed with vendors barking out their sales pitches, while their customers bobbed round looking for a bargain.

John broke off from the rest of the group, to chase after Shirley, who he'd secretly been wanting to kiss for a matter of weeks now. She'd invited him to her twelfth birthday party so that seemed invitation enough for his advances.

As she ran from him, she tittered herself silly, always slipping just out of John's view, just when he thought he might be able to catch her on a straight stretch of road. Their chase continued down a quieter alleyway, away from the main street and all the hustle and bustle of the market. In fact it was deserted. Boarded-up shop fronts and completely devoid of sound. There wasn't even any washing hanging up to dry outside the windows.

A strange sense tingled up John's spine and he came to a halt. He wasn't sure what it had been, a rotten smell in the air perhaps, but there was certainly something wrong with this place. He put the worry to the back of his mind and padded on, after Shirley.

He turned the corner and came face to face with a dead end. He looked up at the blue sky, high above. The houses went up at least seven storeys high—Shirley never could've climbed up there. He glanced back over his shoulder, but he was sure that there was no chance Shirley could've doubled back, shot right past him without him noticing.

That just left the houses. She must've gone inside one of them. But which one? He had a choice of eight or nine doors here. After using his powers of better-than-average deduction he set out to try doors one by one. They were all locked, except the last he tried. When he turned the handle the hinges creaked and the door slapped open against the interior wall.

He lingered on the hearth, recalling all the lessons his parents had drilled into him, about respecting other people's property, asking permission before. But he would be quick. And, anyway, Shirley was being just as bad as him, in fact she was worse because she'd been the one to go inside first. And so he slipped inside, drawing the door closed behind him.

"Shirley?" he called out into the house.

No response. The only sound in the house was

the faint buzz of the market, entering through an open street window.

He inched his way inside, taking stock of his surroundings. Shelves stood on either side. They were stuffed full with bits of twigs, dried flowers, their petals crumbling, and the odd bronze jug. The flowers made his eyes itch, the same sensation he got when he went out into the fields after a harvest. He suppressed a sneeze.

"Hello?" he said. "Where are you, Shirley? We shouldn't be in here."

"I know you shouldn't," someone said from behind him.

John flinched then spun round.

A large woman confronted him. She had jet black hair and several moles covering her cheeks. Her chin was flat and wide, almost occupying the whole base of her jaw. "What're you doing here, in my house?"

John wanted to explain everything, to tell her that he was only here looking for Shirley, but he was too afraid to speak, so he just stood there like an idiot.

"Well?" the woman said, arching an eyebrow.

Still John couldn't find the courage to speak.

"Don't you know what the people of the town call me?"

This time John did find his voice. "I . . . I don't know. I'm only here for the day, my parents just brought me here so I could go to the market. We came with everyone else from my village. I was chasing after one of my friends and she came in here."

The woman stuck out her lower lip. "I haven't seen anyone else."

He looked over her face, not sure whether or not she was telling the truth. Whatever the case might be he was sure that he wanted to get out of the place, right that second. He made for the door. "I'm sorry for coming in here, I was just looking for my friend." He got to the door and tried the handle. It wouldn't move in his grasp. Guessing that it might've got stuck, he put all his weight into turning, but still it wouldn't budge. He turned back to the woman. "I can't get it open."

"I know," the woman said. "I locked it."

"But, how, I . . . I didn't see you—"

"There are ways of locking doors, other than keys."

His blood froze. Witchcraft. What else did she mean? Every impulse told him to run, but where? There was a window behind the woman, the one facing into the market—down below he could hear the energetic cries of the vendors but they seemed so distant now, a world away.

He made a break for the window, rushed round

the woman, who made no effort to grab hold of him. Just as he got within a fingertip's length of the window, it slammed shut, the glass vibrating in the frame. He pressed his nose to the glass and looked down on the market. There, he saw his parents wandering back and forth, searching for him. He shouted out to them but they didn't hear him. Only when he pressed his hands to his throat did he realise the witch had stolen his power of speech.

The witch stepped toward him, holding her head to one side. "The question is, what should I do with such a naughty child? You must be taught a lesson, that's to be taken for granted, but how should I go about it, what would be the most effective way?"

When John attempted to move his arm he saw that it was locked in position, his whole body was stuck in its position. Only in his mind could he scream.

The witch stood right before him now. She reached out with her long nails and tapped him on the forehead. "Can you still hear me in there? Not gone to sleep, have you?"

John simmered within, wanting to break out, attack her, rush from the house.

"Here," she said, twirling her finger in the air. "You can speak for a moment."

It felt like a pair of invisible hands left John's

throat. But when he spoke he could hardly talk above a whisper. "This isn't fair."

The witch cackled. "Do you know what the people of the town would do to me if they found out I was a witch? They would break into my house in the middle of the night, drag me from my bed, and tie me to a stake in the square"—she pointed out the window—"just out there, beyond that stall, and they would burn me alive, screaming and crying out for help. And all that just for being born the way I am. Does that sound fair to you?"

Although he had been told ever since he was a tiny baby that witches had to be got rid of, that they poisoned the earth, brought sickness to townspeople, he knew he had to be shrewd, to play the situation as it unfolded. "No," he said. "No, it doesn't."

"Then you'll sympathise with me for what I'm about to do to you."

The hands round his throat tightened and he was sure she was going to strangle the life out of him. His vision went dim round the edges and he thought he was going to faint. Only, right at the last moment, did the hands relent and, slowly, the world returned to him. He choked to draw breath and he would've fallen to his knees had he been able.

The witch sneered. "Death is almost too good for you, that's what they would do for me. You're just a child after all. Children can learn, or so I'm led to believe." She tapped her finger against her chin in thought then, out of nowhere, snapped her fingers. "I know what I can do for you, how I might be able to aid the learning process." She bowed her head so that her chin almost touched her chest. "It'll take a little time but I think it'll be worth it." She glowered at him, her eyes piercing his and said, "Sleep."

WHEN JOHN CAME BACK ROUND he was surrounded by bars. In a cage. Suspended from the ceiling of the witch's house. As his senses gradually returned to him, he found feeling in his feet again, that he could move all his limbs once more, he got up and clenched his fists round the bars and peered out.

The witch stood below him, her back hunched, mumbling something to herself while a cauldron bubbled away before her. The mixture inside was a purple-brown mulch. It hissed and sighed as she stirred at it.

The mixture wormed its way through the air, up to John's nostrils. It stank of onion and carried the rusty smell of blood. It reminded him of the Sunday lunches his mother would make back home, after he'd been helping his father and his brothers to mend something round the house: a broken roof tile or a gap in one of the walls.

As the house was steeped in darkness now, the only light came from the embers below the cauldron. The witch's face was lit up in the orange glow, her eyes firmly fixed on the wooden spoon which she used to stir the mixture. All of a sudden, the witch turned her gaze upward, to him, smiled. "Wakey, wakey, child. You've got to take your medicine."

John backed away from the bars and crouched down as best he could in the cramped space. He stared out the window, into the street. Although it was impossible to see out he was sure that the market had packed up, that his parents had searched long and hard before giving him up as lost. He had no expectation that they would save him now. No one could save him now. He was in the hands of a witch.

The witch continued to speak things to the mixture in the cauldron. It would respond with bubbles frothing on the surface or sparks flying upward. Every so often she would glance back up at him, that same smug grin on her lips.

What John guessed to be the middle of the night, judging by the moon now filling the window into the street, the witch whipped the cauldron off its peg and hung it to one side, away from the embers. She reached to the side where a pulley was located and she tugged on it.

The cage descended.

John tightened his grip on the bars, knowing that he had to take any chance he could muster to escape her. He wondered why she wasn't holding him captive with her powers, then realised that she must be expending the majority of her magic on whatever potion it was that she was mixing up.

With a snap of the fingers, the witch opened the door to the cage.

Feeling tentative, John held back. Whatever horror she had in store for him it would be better for him just to stay here, in his cage, to put it off for another few precious moments. If he tried to run, even if he caught her off guard, he was sure that she would seize him with her magic long before he reached the door. But he had to try.

Choosing his moment, when the witch had turned her back to inspect some item or other hanging on the shelf, he rushed out of the cage and made for the door. It filled his sight, the doorknob tempting him forward. He surprised himself when he got to the door without the witch stopping him. He looked back at her.

She had the same smile on her lips.

Not wanting to waste his opportunity, he put all his weight into cranking open the door, but it remained stiff. He should have known she would keep a hold on the door.

The witch plucked a the plant she'd taken down off the shelf, scattering its parts onto the top layer of the potion. "I might not have the strength to keep you still but I can prevent you from leaving. Didn't your parents ever warn you about entering a witch's house, that you'd need her permission before you'd be allowed to leave?"

It was just about the first thing his mother had told him, as soon as he'd been able to understand rules. He was sure it had followed soon after the rule about not touching fire or putting his hand in boiling water. And yet he had been stupid enough to fall for it, to get himself into a life-threatening situation.

Panicked, he beat his fists against the door and cried out, hoping that someone passing by or a neighbour might hear him.

The witch chuckled. "You might find you'll have better luck at the window on the other side, the one that faces out into the street. Everyone moved away from this area a long time ago, decided that it was poxed: children being born with feet instead of hands, hands instead of feet. They said it was something in the water, that someone had placed a curse on this place."

"You did it to them!"

"What a perceptive young man you are."

Despite the witch's claims, he continued to punch the door and yowl. Someone must be able to hear him, he was sure of it. Maybe they had heard the cries once too often, perhaps they no longer responded to the odd sounds coming from this house. Or was it, like his mother had told him, that the witch had created some kind of protective aura so that nothing ever wilfully left.

She closed her eyes and hummed to herself. "Now that the potion's ready, I feel my strength returning. That should make things much easier for both of us." She raised her arms above her head and continued her incantations.

John's chest tightened and he felt his feet moving beneath him, against his will. He sucked in a breath, to let loose one final cry, one last plea for help, but when he tried his throat was dry and he was back within the hold of those familiar invisible hands.

The hands walked him across the floor of the house, right up to the cauldron, where the witch was already dipping her wooden spoon into the mixture, bringing it up to her nose to sniff. He wanted to resist but no matter how hard he tried he was stiff as a plank.

The witch gazed down into the spoon, the mixture puddled there. She brought it up to John's lips. His head tilted back, the invisible hands again, and his mouth opened wide. The mixture slopped into his mouth, burnt his tongue, but John had no way of announcing his pain. It slipped down his throat, through his chest and, finally, nestled in his stomach where it swirled, as if it had created some kind of whirlpool there.

The witch withdrew, dropped the spoon back in the cauldron. She gazed at the mixture. "Well, I'd better bottle some of this, some of my finest work, if I do say so myself." She turned back to John. "As for you, I think you'd better go have a nap in your cage. I promise you'll feel much better when you wake up."

3

DESPITE THE WITCH'S claims that he would sleep, John found it impossible. The liquid surged inside him, as it biting through each of his internal organs one by one, turning them inside-out, upside-down. The motion reminded him of when he would watch his mother knead dough in the kitchen, her fists going in and out, folding it over and crushing it with her palms.

The worst of the process was the tiny cage, seemingly closing in on him with each of the internal wrenches. He wanted to burst out, bend the bars, just make himself more comfortable. The witch wanted him to suffer as badly as she knew how.

Only when sunlight penetrated the window, draped itself over the house, with all its crooked angles and shelves stuffed full of jars of preserved potions, did his stomach begin to feel any better. He felt round him, the cage still surrounding him, and noticed his hands.

They had grown to about five times their original size. His thumbs resembled pickles, his fingers blood sausages, the kind that the travellers sometimes brought through the village to sell. He had to crane his neck so as to fit inside the cage. His legs snaked out beneath him, thick and unwieldy. No longer could he move at all. He was reduced to staring out into the house, to waiting for the witch to return to free him.

The witch arrived a little later, stifling a yawn, wearing a dressing gown, apparently made of silk. She peered upward at him, clapped her hands together. "My, my, my, you've really transformed wonderfully, if I do say so myself." She approached the pulley and brought the cage down. "Now, you must promise me that you'll behave yourself if I let you out."

John had no intention of behaving himself.

She snapped her fingers and the cage door squeaked open.

Like a wild animal let loose, John burst from the cage, making straight for the witch's throat. This time he reached her, without being stopped by her powers. He took hold of her skin, trapping it and tightening his grip.

Her eyes bulged in their sockets.

As he stared into her eyes, knowing that he was killing her, a doubt entered his thinking. He knew that this was a witch, but could he really kill her, just like that?

Somehow, the witch seemed to take advantage of his momentary hesitation and those invisible hands returned, taking hold of *his* throat, sending him stumbling back.

He tripped over the cage and fell back, onto his bottom.

The witch loomed above him, her eyes sharp and lips pressed tightly together. She lurched forward, murmuring words in a language John didn't understand, then said, "Now you shall suffer just as I did. You can be cast away from the rest of civilisation, you can be a monster."

There was a flash of bright, white light. The room dimmed to a shadow and the world spun round and round. The walls flung themselves away.

John scrabbled to get a grip on the world tearing itself apart, but there was nothing to hold onto. He had no choice but to surrender himself to the whirlwind and where it would leave him.

4

FINALLY, the movement came to a halt. Birds sang. Crickets chirped. In the distance, a wolf howled.

John opened his eyes. He was sitting in the middle of a pasture. He recognised the place. It was the field behind his house—his father's field. Up ahead he saw his house. It looked so inviting from where he sat, like the nightmare reality of the witch's house had left him behind and now he was back to real life.

His whole body ached and his skin felt sore. He examined his deformed hands, arms and legs. He wanted to get a look at the rest of his body, his face. Casting off his body's complaints, he stood and made his way through the field, the long wheat swaying against his hips. Before his transformation, the wheat had towered over his head.

He arrived at the back porch of the house, where he had sat so often in the evenings, with all his brothers round him, listening to them tell stories. His father was the best storyteller. He would hold forth in his wicker rocking chair, pipe in mouth, smoking away, and regale them with stories of his childhood— where he claimed he'd been a brave sword-for-hire, and he'd gone off slaying dragons, liberating gold and rescuing princesses. He often claimed that their mother had been one such princess who, tired of the high-life, had accepted his marriage proposal, and come to live with him here.

John lingered at the porch door and then pushed his way inside.

His mother stood with her back to him, chopping vegetables at the kitchen table, popping them into a pot hanging over the stove as she went.

Those same oniony smells reminded John of the potion. His stomach churned at the thought. He slunk back into the kitchen, afraid to speak. He had no need to, though, because a few seconds later his mother turned.

She gawped at him, her mouth flapping open and shut like a banked fish.

John tried to speak but his vocal cords felt large and unwieldy, and all he could get out was a groan.

His mother let loose a blood curdling cream. She sent vegetables flying as she snatched up the knife and wagged it through the air. "Don't you dare come any closer, you monster. How in the gods' name did you get in here, that's what I want to know!"

John said something which he hoped would be, "I came in through the back porch," but only a series of groans, one melding into the next, emerged from his lips.

Footsteps sounded in the house, boots hustling toward the kitchen.

John surveyed his options. It was better to get out of the house, come back later, when everything had calmed down, once he'd worked out how to use his vocal cords. He tried to back up, but he bumped into the kitchen wall. He felt for the door and brought one of the exterior walls tumbling down in a stream of dust and plaster.

"Get out!" his mother said, waggling the knife at him.

John's father and his two oldest brothers, Hickory and Smith, arrived in the doorway. They absorbed him with their eyes and, for a moment, John was certain he saw some recognition there. But it was lost to fear. His father unsheathed the scabbard he kept on his belt and rushed for John.

With no way of escaping, John was reduced to ducking and weaving, keeping his father's blade from nicking his skin. Once, though, it did catch him, just beneath the chin. Warm blood trickled down his throat. And then, backed into a corner, his father holding the blade up high, and John's two older brothers now clutching kitchen knives at his shoulder, John let loose a roar and batted his father out of the way with his enormous arm.

His father flew through the air and smashed into the opposite wall. As he slid down to the floor, John noted the large dent his form had left there.

His brothers didn't step into the fray, too taken off guard by John's show of strength.

Before John had to fight again, he bounded out of the kitchen, back through the porch door and into the fields. Now it was too late for him to return. As he escaped, his brothers would be whipping the villagers into a frenzy, telling them to grab their weapons and accompany them to slay the beast that had invaded their home. And who could blame them? In the same situation, John would've done the same.

He took in the Damned Forests, spread out on the hillside up ahead, and he made for them. When he had been just a twelve-year-old boy he would never have dreamt of entering, but now, now that he was a monster, his fear seemed to have deserted him.

Trees sprung up on either side. He kept up his same pace, his strides at least five times those of his twelve-year-old self. He continued until the light in the forest waned and his muscles felt ragged and ready to rest. He reached a clearing and collapsed onto the ground made soft by decomposing pine needles, leaning up against a fallen log.

Now he had some time to think, he thought about his father. He wondered how badly he had hurt him. If he had broken a bone that would impact his family terribly. His father wouldn't be able to work, he would have to delegate his duties to his brothers and, although they were young, they were stupid, and often did things wrong—just as their father would always point out. And what if John had killed him?

A heavy tear rolled down the side of John's nose. He wiped it away with his large paw. It didn't bear thinking about. He held his head between his kneecaps, feeling a chill creep up on him. Where was he going to go now that he had left his family behind? He had no idea about how to survive out here in the wild—less so in the Damned Forest.

Somewhere behind him there was a rustling.

He jerked his head round to see. But, it being near dark, he could hardly make out the hand in front of his face, let alone some animal in the underbrush.

Another rustle directly in front of him.

He backed up against the log. Whatever was out there, there were several of them and they were working together, closing a circle round him. He tried to give himself courage, telling himself that although the witch had deformed him horribly, she'd also given him great strength. He could defend himself if he only kept his mind alert.

And then a rustle to his right, to his left, then the whole forest seemed to come alive with sounds of animals moving against foliage.

All confidence left him. He really had no chance against this large a number, no matter how strong he was. He just made himself as small as possible, like what his father said he should do if he ever came up against a honey boar, or other predator, out in the field.

There was a flicker of a flame. It steadied and moved through the darkness. Then others twinkled into light and there were dozens of flames all surrounding him. As his eyes adjusted to the gloom, he realised that they were candles, and the candles illuminated faces.

One drew close to him.

John gasped.

It was a man, how old he couldn't say. His entire face was covered in wrinkles, layers and layers of skin, no features. He had to hold the wrinkles back to see through one eye. He stalked closer, hobbling slightly, he held the candle up to John's face then made a strange croaking noise.

Only after John had got his fear under control did he realise that the man was laughing—or trying to.

A woman, totally covered in yellow hair, sidled up alongside the man. "Who've we got here, then?"

An older man arrived at John's elbow. He had no idea what might be wrong with him until he opened his mouth and saw he had hundreds of tongues. They wriggled like snakes as he spoke, enunciating slowly. "You . . . with . . . the . . . witch . . . too?"

John managed a nod.

The woman reached out to touch his cheek. "Oh, you poor dear. Just like the rest of us. Damned by black magic." She turned round to address the others, dozens and dozens of them, filling the clearing. "Give us some room here, will you?"

There seemed to be no change in the spread of the candles, if anything they came closer, shining more and more light over John.

When John attempted to speak, he found he still couldn't. He pounded his fist against the ground in frustration.

The woman laid a hand on his shoulder. "Don't worry, dear, you'll be fine with us. We'll teach you to talk, everything like that, lots of us had problems when we got here—but we help each other out." She squeezed his shoulder. "We're you're family now."

John took in all the faces staring down at him, so many deformities, it was hard to believe that they had all gone through similar stories as him, that they had all suffered at the hand of witchcraft. He supposed they had all lost his families, just like him, been outcast.

"Someone help him up," the woman said.

Several hands helped John to his feet.

He allowed them to lift him, aware of the strain, all the effort it took them to raise up his large body. Once he was back on his feet he much felt better, lucky to have found these people—people just like him.

They all guided him through the night forest. He trusted them completely. Their lights glowed through the darkness, making everything seem more familiar, even warm. They kept on going until the woman, who seemed to be something of a ringleader, stopped him outside an especially large tree. She rested a reas-suring arm on his and then prodded at a knot on the tree trunk. A door creaked out from the bark and, beyond that, a stairway lit by torches.

"This is our home," she said. "Witney Branches." She took a deep breath. "Now, dear, you're going to have to make a choice. Are you going to come and live with us?"

Unable to speak, he merely nodded.

She looked back to the crowd. "Did you all hear that? He's one of us now." She turned back to John and grinned. "One of the Grotesque."

PRINCE COURTNEY

ALEXIS PROWLED along the school corridor, trying her best to block out all the crap that was spewing from Prince Courtney's mouth. Goodness, did he have a mouth on him. She really had no idea how this friendship had sprung up. All she'd been doing was minding her own business in maths, when he had suddenly decided that he was going to speak to her. And, pretty soon after *he* had started the conversation, he demanded that she refer to him as Prince Courtney, not just Courtney—as if Courtney wouldn't be ridiculous enough on its own.

As she reached the stairwell, knowing that Courtney had to go up, to get to science, just as she had to go along the corridor, to French, she came to a halt. She put on what was fast becoming her painful separation face. "Sorry, Courtney—"

He held up his hand. "We've been over this, Alexis."

"I meant, Prince Courtney."

"Better," he said, with a regal nod.

"Looks like we've got to go our separate ways here."

He blinked a couple of times at her then said,

"Alexis, I've been thinking. How would you like to come on a little adventure with me?"

Alexis knew one thing from lines that included 'little adventure' sprouting from the mouths of boys. It generally meant going back to their bedroom, or your bedroom, it really made no difference.

While she had to admit that Courtney wasn't without his charms, what with the washboard stomach or his neck-length, crisp, wavy blond hair that she'd just love to tear her fingers through or . . . she was only fooling herself, really, it didn't matter that Courtney blabbered his brains out, it didn't change the fact he was insanely attractive.

"Alexis? Alexis? Earth to Alexis?" he said, holding his finger to his ear and pretending to speak into an invisible microphone clipped to his t-shirt. "So, what do you say?"

Returning from her daydreaming, it was all she could do to clutch her books to her chest. "Uh, about what?"

"The adventure."

"Um, okay."

Courtney burst into a gleaming smile.

It was one of those smiles so perfect that she could just tell that he'd never had any dental work done—no matter how good the dentist, work always leaves some trace, some imperfections. Sometimes she wondered whether he was from this planet at all.

". . . Alexis? Alexis?"

Again, she'd missed out a paragraph-long diatribe. "Sorry, I kind of zoned out there."

Courtney huffed a short sigh. "All right, you're in, okay?"

"Yeah, I guess."

"Good," Courtney said, snatching her by the wrist and twisting her round, so that they were headed for the exit.

Above their heads the second bell rang. The bell announcing the start of the lesson.

"Wha—where are we going?" Alexis said.

"Like I just told you, we have to go now."

Alexis dug her heels in, brought them to a complete stop in the hallway. "I can't just leave school. I haven't missed a lesson in my life."

Courtney rolled his eyes. "Look, I gave you the choice, you said yes, now, are you coming or not?" He caught her in his laser-blue eyes. "Or are you going to disappoint me, Alexis?"

Alexis glanced off along the corridor, trying to ascertain whether or not a teacher had seen them out of class, that would save her—a teacher could shout some sense into Courtney. But, just like a policeman, there were never teachers around when needed.

Courtney jerked her toward the exit with a smile. "Oh, good, let's get a move on then."

Alexis peered back at the disappearing school doors, thinking about her perfect attendance record going out the window. It would've taken something absolutely, totally exceptional to cause her to miss a class and, as fate would have it, Prince Courtney was just that.

2

THEY PACED along the street, Alexis still trying to catch her breath, to tell herself that she was really here, outside of school, while there was a lesson that she was supposed to be in. This was just about the worst thing she had ever done in her life. She wondered whether that might be quite sad, and she decided that it probably was.

When they got to a park, Courtney stopped, faced up to her and placed a hand on either of her shoulders. "Alexis, I want you to be my princess. Please say yes."

Alexis really had no idea how to respond. Was he asking her out? Some kind of kooky way to do it, take her out of school, bring her to some park. Not even a particularly nice park. Why couldn't he just have waited until after school?

"Alexis?" he said, a tone of impatience creeping into his voice.

She managed a flicker of a smile. "Uh, okay."

"Good," Courtney said, dragging her back alongside her. "Then we shall return to the Kingdom at once."

"What? We're already in the Kingdom."

Courtney chuckled. "Oh, no, not this. The United

Kingdom's no kingdom I want to be a part of, trust me." He threw back his head and shouted, "Call this a monarchy?" He became serious. "No, Alexis, what you must understand is that I'm an outcast, an exile. I am not here, in your world, by choice, but merely because there's a usurper on the throne, a certain Uncle Fredrick." He screwed up his features in obvious distaste. "Now, my father sent me here to be safe, so that good old Uncle Fred wouldn't murder me in my cot, nothing like that. So, now I'm older, old enough, to go make a play for the throne, I must take my chance." He grinned at her. "And what would I be without a beautiful queen at my side?"

That final comment caught Alexis as something of a sideswipe, almost caused her to completely forget the unchecked guff which had preceded it. In fact it did. "You think I'm beautiful?"

"Oh my, yes," he said, a glimmer in his eye. "But there'll be time for smooches and loving making beneath the stars on balconies a thousand feet up in the air later. First we must hatch a plan to dethrone the evil Uncle Fredrick."

"Right," Alexis said, the weight of what Courtney was saying beginning to seep in. Finally. "Uh, where are we going exactly?"

"Ethereal?"

"Where?"

Courtney flapped his hands. "You'll see, you'll see."

They arrived outside Rutsley Church and Burial Grounds. Alexis put a up a little resistance, to read the sign, and then allowed Courtney to drag her on. She'd come this far so she might as well go a little further.

Shale stones decorated the exterior wall of the church. They rounded it and arrived at one of the buttresses where there was a plaque. It looked as if it had once been black, but the elements had got to it so much so that it was now more of a dark-green colour.

Courtney clasped Alexis's hand tight and brought it up to touch the plaque. There was a layer of mould hanging onto it, so it was a little damp. Alexis tried to yank her hand back, but Courtney kept her hand pressed there. "Really, my dear," he said. "You're going to have to trust me."

Every time Alexis looked over her shoulder for somewhere to run, snapped to her senses that Courtney was in fact a complete nutcase, she found herself ensnared once again in his blindingly-good looks. And so she put up with him holding her hand against the plaque.

At first nothing at all happened, and then the whole world seemed to bleed at the corners, the ground below her feet disintegrated, and all that had once seemed so solid took on the density and complexity of jelly. She wriggled her hand from Courtney's grasp, but it was too late. She had left her world behind.

Although when she looked round they still stood in Rutsley Church and Burial Grounds, the entire sky had changed colour, taken on a purple hue, like the light just before dawn. But, somehow, Alexis got the impression that dawn was never coming.

Gravestones stretched out as far as she could see, into an incalculably expansive vista. They just went on and on. Before she got the chance to interrogate Courtney as to their surroundings, she found herself being whisked away once more, this time between the gravestones.

Alexis caught the eye of a midget, with a mop of white-blond hair, he merely glanced up at her, before returning to his work, scrubbing at a gravestone. She was about to ask Courtney what this midget was about, but, once more, she was whisked away, this time down a narrow row of gravestones and through a rickety wooden gate.

Courtney brought them to a stop by one of the gravestones, looked round then said, "Have you got your stomach back?"

"My stomach?"

"Yes, after the transition, the trip here."

"I . . . I didn't really feel much. Anyway where's—"

But Courtney seized her hand, held it in his and they were touching the gravestone.

Once more the familiar sinking feeling, the whole world breaking apart round them, absorbed Alexis. She shut her eyes and when she opened them once more she was surrounded by green pastures. The air smelled sweeter, fresher, and she realised that it had never been polluted with exhaust fumes. This place, where Courtney had brought her now, was a totally new world.

She stood still, taking in the panorama, the snow-capped mountains in the distance, a clear blue lake in the foreground. To her left was a lush forest of green trees. She looked to Courtney for some kind of explanation, but he was already busy, looking round for something.

Courtney held his hand up to shield his eyes from the blazing sun. He squinted into the distance.

"What just happened?" Alexis said.

Courtney continued looking for another few seconds, glanced at her, and then seemed to twig that she might like something by the way of an explanation. As he explained, he looked distracted still searching for whatever it was he was searching for. "We took a little journey, to The End of Time, then we touched a gravestone, and that brought us here."

Despite everything else, Alexis lost herself again in Courtney's impossible eyes. But, this time, she managed to get over her awe long enough to probe deeper. "Whoa, wait. The End of Time?"

"Yeah."

"It's a graveyard?"

"Yeah."

"And it's at Rutsley Church?"

"Yeah."

"You mean to say that time, as we know it, ends at Rutsley Church?"

Courtney frowned. "Time in your world, in any case. For us, from the other worlds, it just works as a nice little junction, somewhere for us to transport between various worlds."

Alexis caught her breath for several seconds then said, more quietly, "And which world are we in now?"

"Goodness," he said. "You're not very quick on the uptake, are you?"

Alexis knew she should take that as an insult, but, the combination of Courtney's dashing aura and her genuine confusion about what was going on, she could only feel her thoughts clanging round her skull.

Courtney picked out a point on the horizon, shut one eye and stared at it. "We're in Ethereal, like I said. This is my world." He returned his gaze to her and smiled. "Do you like it?"

"It's . . . it's," Alexis said, "beautiful."

Another sparkle shone in his eye. "It is quite, isn't it?" He took hold of her hand and guided her across the pasture. "I think we might be able to find ourselves some horses up ahead, and supplies for our journey."

"Our journey?"

"Look, we're not going to get anywhere with you asking me to recap and revise every three seconds, so I suggest that you just hang about on my heels, looking your gorgeous self, and leave all the adventuring to me."

Again, an instinct bade her to slap him across his milky-white cheeks, but she just couldn't bring herself to do it. She wondered whether she was in love with him, if he had, perhaps, slipped her some kind of love potion. Then she checked herself. She might be standing here, in a supposedly new world, but it was surely more likely that he might've slipped her some kind of drug. She would have to stay on her guard. If that were even possible with those eyes lasering her at every opportunity.

They trudged through knee-high grass for about an hour before they reached a shack. A snorting sound of horses came from round back.

A hunchback with a knot-shaped bruise on his forehead appeared, writhing a dirtied cloth between his hands. "Yeah?" he said.

Courtney put on a smug smile. "Afternoon, commoner, we would like to commandeer two of your finest horses."

The hunchback glanced between them, took a little too long with his eyes lingering on Alexis's chest, then said, "Ain't got none."

"Don't lie, dear commoner, or you might wake up one morning with your head detached from your body. In a permanent way."

Alexis was a little shocked at Courtney's threat. She gave him a sidelong glance.

He leant into her, and dropped his voice to a conspiratorial tone. "Haven't had much practice in insulting commoners in your world, that sort of thing's frowned upon in your time. Hopefully this'll do the trick, though."

Instead, however, the hunchback spat on the dusty ground and, from within his robe, withdrew a scabbard. He swished it through the air a couple of times, for effect, then said, "I'll give you ten seconds to beat it, before I cut *your* heads off."

Courtney puffed out his chest, titled his head upward and said, "Please, peasant, you must remember who you're speaking too. Do you not recognise me? I am the deposed Prince Courtney, rightful heir to the throne of all Ethereal."

"Yeah?" the hunchback said, flashing his eyebrows, then glancing over at Alexis. "Never heard of you. And if you are a royal then what're you doing on foot out here in the sticks? Got any way to prove it?"

Courtney blew out his cheeks, looked round, as if this were a genuine conundrum, and one which he had never anticipated he might face. Then he snapped round. "I tell you what," he said. "Have you got another of those scabbards?"

"No, only this one," the hunchback said.

"Drat."

Alexis wondered whether she should step in, offer her two cents, but she really had no idea what kind of thing would pass for evidence out here. Then she did come up with something. Giving Courtney an unsure look, she stepped forward, toward the hunchback, holding her hands up in surrender, in the hope he wouldn't slice her head off. "Um, how about if Prince Courtney swears he's the true king to the gods, or something?"

The hunchback looked over Alexis, then back to Courtney. He pouted, sheathed his scabbard, but kept hold of the hilt. "All right," he said.

Prince Courtney clapped his hands together in

delight, then glanced at Alexis. "Now that really is out-of-the-box thinking, I knew I chose my bride well." He turned back to the hunchback. "Yes, peasant, I swear that I am the rightful king, the true king, to the gods."

The hunchback snorted. "All right. Don't want to anger the gods, or nuffink." He gave the sky a cursory glance as if some hand might jab down through the clouds and smush him right where he stood. "Horses you want, eh? I'll give you my two best, like you asked."

While the hunchback disappeared round his shack to saddle up the horses, Courtney turned on Alexis, looked deep into her eyes and then took her in his arms. He pressed his lips to hers and kissed heavily, and long, his tongue worming against hers.

Alexis's heart bobbed in her throat and she thought she might faint. She was only saved by the impatient cough of the hunchback who stood, dour-faced, holding two horses by their reins. He gave them one each, muttered some unintelligible curse beneath his breath and retreated to his shack.

NEVER HAVING TOUCHED a horse before, let along have ridden one, Alexis's whole body ached at the end of the day's ride. Courtney brought them to a halt beside a burbling stream, tying the horses to a busted-up log sticking out of the earth. He used the saddles to give them a comfortable seat and they rested there, staring up at the stars.

Here, in Ethereal, the stars were so much brighter, each of them like a spotlight, beaming down on them. Alexis wished she could bottle the essence of this place, take it back home with her. And then the thought struck here. Would she ever get to go home?

"Erm, Courtney—?"

Courtney gave her a look of warning.

"Prince Courtney, I mean, I was just wondering, when will we be going back to the normal world?"

"'Normal? Normal?'" He snickered. "Yes, I suppose *that* place is normal for you, though how anyone manages to live their entire life there really defeats me."

"Well, it's my home."

Courtney shook his head. "Oh no, my dear, this is

your home now. When I've retained the throne you shall sit by my side, be my queen, and we shall rule over the land, oh-so benevolently."

Alexis considered mentioning the fact that he had just cheated a peasant out of a horse, but decided it better not to bring it up. Considering Courtney would be her ticket home it was best not to anger him. She had no idea what kinds of people, or creatures, inhabited this world. Courtney was her guide.

Later on, Courtney complained of hunger and disappeared off down to the stream. He returned a few minutes later with half a dozen fish on sticks, his trousers rolled up just above his calves. He made a fire in a matter of minutes and soon fish juice was spitting against the embers, the rich scent coiling through the air, sending waves of hunger through Alexis. Perhaps she had underestimated Courtney— maybe there was more to him than just dashing good looks.

4

THE NEXT DAY they rode on. Alexis's whole body had gone stiff overnight and it felt like she was going to burst at the seams at any moment. But Courtney set such a frantic pace that she had no opportunity to complain. During the ride, when she wasn't concentrated on her pain, she wondered what was happening back in her world—whether anyone was missing her. She rode up alongside Courtney and asked him.

Courtney chuckled. "My goodness, you really are green when it comes to this travelling-between-worlds lark, aren't you?"

"Well, yeah, I've never done it before."

Courtney turned his hand over and examined his nails. "No, no one will miss you. For all intents and purposes your world has frozen, it won't move on an inch while we're here."

"But how—"

"Ethereal is a far superior world, you see. For every one of your Earth seconds, Ethereal passes decades, centuries, I'm not sure which, I never had a particular talent for mathematics."

With those looks, Alexis supposed he really didn't need to have a talent for anything. And, if it was true that he was from a royal bloodline in this world, then it held that he really needn't bother himself with the business of mere mortals.

They rode on and on, and on. This time they didn't bother stopping to sleep at night, or to eat. She had always wondered how Courtney kept himself so thin, and now she knew. The boy had resolve, she had to give him that.

When the next morning dawned, Courtney trotted them through the remainder of some woods and, against all odds, brought their ride to a halt. He got down off his horse, stripped some berries from the tree and handed them over to Alexis.

Although she consciously told herself not to make a spectacle of her hunger, not to munch her way through these offerings with all the grace of the pig, when it came down to the crunch, she was really starving. So she did gorge herself.

Once she was through with the berries, she looked round expectantly for more food. A spit-roasted pig would've been welcome after that starter.

Courtney seemed to sense her hunger. He only smiled his big, perfect smile while he patted the neck of Alexis's horse. "Don't worry, my sweet, when the pretender has fallen from the throne, I shall hold several banquets in your honour. Never again shall you feel the pangs of hunger."

That did sound reassuring.

"Now," Courtney said, looking off into the distance and pointing. "Over there, do you see? Rising out of the mist?"

Alexis took a long hard look and, just on the horizon, she made out the shape of a large structure. As the sun burnt through layers of mist, she noticed the turrets and then, another few moments later, she could pick out the moat, the drawbridge. "Is . . . is that a castle?"

Courtney beamed. "Yes. That is the home of my rightful throne." He narrowed his eyes. "And that's where Uncle Fredrick sits, no doubt laughing at my misfortune every morning, enjoying every second of his stolen rule."

For the first time in their relationship, Alexis sensed some real ice in Courtney's tone. He really did want to get the throne back, like this was the most important moment of his life. She supposed, if she'd been in his shoes, she would've felt similar. Except she guessed that out here, in Ethereal, queens were tolerated rather than embraced. For all Courtney's flag-flying for this world, she still saw the benefits of her world—it having passed through the more rudimentary modes of feminism.

As if Courtney had an eye to her thoughts, he slapped her on the thigh, told her to hide herself in the undergrowth and that, all being well, he would return by nightfall, the new King of Ethereal.

At this, Alexis had to object. "I'm coming with you."

Courtney laughed. "Impossible. War and women don't mix."

She fumed to herself, this time managing to side-step the devastating good looks. "I might just surprise you. Remember with the hunchback and the horses?"

Courtney did appear to turn this over in his mind. He looked off into the distance, as if he had some kind of x-ray vision, and he was sizing up the defences. When he glanced back at her, he said, "You may be right, my sweet. Perhaps you would be a useful addition to my party." He pursed his lips. "But I must warn you that if this fight doesn't go as planned then I may not be able to make provisions for what becomes of you."

A knot stuck in Alexis's throat. Now she really was regretting being a woman in Ethereal. But, if she backed down now, she would seem like a coward, and she was determined to teach Courtney a lesson or two.

So they rode out across the plain, the castle looming up ahead of them. With each *clop* of hoof, Alexis was sure that it grew in size, that it became more and more imposing. When they reached the drawbridge, Courtney called up to a sentry watching them approach from the turret. "What ho!"

"Who goes there?" the sentry said.

"Prince Courtney, and his bride-to-be, the true successor to the Throne of Ethereal."

There was a pause while the sentry seemed to deliberate with someone else. He appeared back up in the space above the drawbridge. "What do you want?"

Courtney stiffened his shoulders. "I *want* the opportunity to reclaim my throne, to take back what is truly mine, to depose the pretender, King Fredrick."

More deliberation from above the drawbridge.

They waited what seemed to be an impossibly long time and Alexis was just about to suggest that they return to the forest when the drawbridge chains clanked and cogs churned. The drawbridge descended before their eyes, coming to a rest with a *thud* as it met the damp ground at their feet.

Courtney flashed a smile at Alexis.

Warmth flushed through her stomach, Courtney's good looks still, somehow, overcoming her apprehension. She wondered how long his hold on her would last. Perhaps until his death, which might well be hopping right along at any moment.

Another sentry popped up beside the first and they watched on as Courtney and Alexis proceeded along the drawbridge. Alexis was a little perturbed to hear the *creak* of wood beneath her feet, guessing that health and safety remained just as uninvented as feminism—maybe if Courtney's coup went off without a hitch she might float some of these concepts.

They arrived in a walled courtyard. As they dismounted, tied their horses up to what seemed to be visitors' horse parking, Alexis tilted her head upward where she noted the crossbowmen all standing on the turrets, looking down them, their weapons primed. She nudged Courtney. "Uh, have you seen them?"

Courtney gave her a reassuring smile—or was there *some* trace of nerves back there somewhere? "Don't worry! We're inside now, that was the hard part."

A pair of guards, each armed with a spear, arrived before them. One said, "So you are the man who would challenge our king?"

Courtney smirked. "I am your king."

The guards nonchalantly exchanged glances, perhaps they had seen something similar to this play out before.

"Now," Courtney said, "lead me to the court so I may challenge the usurper to a fight to the death."

The guard who had spoken before made some sort of gesture to one of the crossbowmen up on the wall who, in turn, made his way into the castle, no doubt to consult someone more senior on the matter.

While they waited, an uncomfortable silence draped over them. Never having liked suffering awkward silences, Alexis took it upon herself to break through it. "Is the weather always this lovely round this time of year?"

The guard gave her a blank look. "You talk funny."

When the crossbowman returned he gave the guard a curt nod.

The guard waved his spear in Courtney and Alexis's faces and then steered them along a winding stone corridor. Alexis noted the ever-changing gradient beneath their feet. No real engineering forethought to boast of either. With every new experience in Ethereal, she was doubting Courtney's judgement of it being far superior to Earth.

They arrived in the court where several men and women stood about, all dressed in garishly-coloured clothes. And everyone seemed to be wearing buckles, whether they were tied round their elbows, or round the backs of their knees. Alexis supposed it must've been a sort of fad.

There was a portly man perched on the edge of the throne. He wore a lime-green tunic and was resting his head on his hand, gazing out the window, as if he would rather have been anywhere else. The aforementioned King Fredrick.

When the two of them were announced by the guardsmen, the King perked up, looked them over, his mouth curling at the corners, slowly trans-forming into a wry smile. "What have we here?" he said.

Alexis had no intention of making waves in this court. She didn't particularly want her head to end up on the pointy end of a pike, or to be burnt as a witch, for that matter.

Courtney stepped forward, holding his head high. He batted his fringe from his eyes. "Uncle, it is I, Courtney."

Fredrick wrinkled his brow. "Courtney?"

"You might not remember me. I am your broth-er's son, and I was smuggled out of Ethereal as a baby so that you would not slay me while I still suckled at my mother's breast."

Alexis wondered whether that addition might've been a little extraneous.

Still Fredrick looked puzzled. He waved to one of

his aides, standing close at his side. "Jenson, is this man any relation to me?"

Jenson trod forward so he stood only inches from Courtney then squinted into his face. "No, sire, I don't believe so."

Fredrick's expression darkened another tone or two.

Courtney opened his mouth to speak, but, before he had the chance to get the words out three separate blades brushed his throat.

Alexis noticed one of the women of the court had arrived at her side and produced her own blade which she also held to her throat.

Fredrick rose out of his throne, stepped up close to Courtney, so that their noses were only a matter of inches apart. He let loose a growl from the base of his throat. "You are a liar, I'm sure of it. I know for a fact that my brother never had a son. But, as I'm in a appeasing mood, I'll let you live. For the time being." He stepped back, toward his throne. He rested a hand on the arm. For high treason, the failure to duly bow down before the right and truthful King of Ethereal, I hereby banish you to the dungeons for twenty years. Both of you!"

A breath hitched in Alexis's throat. Before she had time to fully absorb what had just happened, she found herself being led away from the court, the same woman holding the dagger to her throat, the blade nipping at her skin.

As the guards led him before her, Courtney managed to look back over his shoulder, even managing a smile. "Nothing to worry about, my sweet. Just a minor setback."

They headed down a set of spiral stairs. The light grew dim, as the pathway ahead was only lit by torches. Alexis guessed that they must be several feet below the castle by now. Already she could smell the rusty scent of blood.

They descended further still, until the ground levelled out and they proceeded along a narrow and low-ceilinged corridor. Alexis and her escort had to duck to make their way through.

And then the cells appeared in view. Thick iron bars prevented entrance or egress. One of the guards opened the squeaking door and then hurled them both through the gap, before slamming it shut behind them.

Alexis landed with a soft *thump* on some straw— clearly several days old from the stench. She propped herself up to watch Courtney remonstrating with the bored-looking guards, to no visible end. She turned her attention to look through the gloom, to another prisoner there, sitting on the floor, staring at his toes.

He had a bald head that retained a shine, even down here.

The prisoner turned to face her. "So what've you done to get put down here?"

"My companion is the true King of Ethereal."

"Is that so?"

"Why don't you ask him yourself?"

The prisoner took stock of Courtney. "Nah, you're all right, he looks like a mental case, to me."

"Hey!" Courtney said, turning away from the bars. "I heard that!" He stooped over the prisoner. "Tell me, knave, what is your name?"

The prisoner let loose a sigh, gave Alexis a knowing glance then said, "My name's Sydney, but almost everyone round here calls me the Bald Poet."

Alexis hunched her knees up to her chest. "Well, it looks like we'll be stuck down here, for the time being."

Courtney paced back and forth. "We need a plan, that's all. Excellent really to get this opportunity to think. Now I'm sure to be King!"

Alexis groaned internally and, in her mind, rehashed how exactly she had managed to end up here, in some sort of medieval prison when she had been in school just that morning. She had fallen for Courtney's charms and now, surely, he would get her killed—painfully and slowly.

DIVUS & DORIS

DIVUS HOCKED UP an enormous wad of phlegm and spat onto the gravestone. He yanked the cloth from the waistband of his trousers and, tongue sticking out the corner of his mouth, scrubbed away at the marble. After several minutes he had somewhat loosened the external layer of grease and muck, and he was making headway with the more profoundly stuck-on grime.

Over his shoulder, a couple dressed in Tudor costume appeared out of thin air, beside a gravestone. They looked red-faced, hair all over the place, like they'd just run the gauntlet in one place or another. Most likely they had.

Divus applied fresh spit to the gravestone and gave it a final rub, already anticipating the inevitable.

The Tudor gentleman approached, wide-eyed his frilly-necked shirt torn down to his belly button. There was a nasty gash just below his nipple. He had a slight limp. "Midget, pray, where are we?"

If there was one thing which really got Divus's goat—apart from being stuck here for all eternity—it was starry-eyed humans, leaping their way between one world and the next. Nonetheless, with infinite patience, Divus met the man's eye. "You're at The End of Time."

"The what?" he said, gawking.

Divus returned his dirtied cloth to his waistband. "The. End. Of. Time."

"This?" the man said, still unbelieving. "This can't be—"

But then his gaze wandered behind him, to the gravestones which stretched on for infinity, every human who had ever lived. A light mist was settling in over the landscape so it wasn't possible to see the very caps of the mountains. Divus was glad because, despite his magical powers, the instant teleportation, he had no intention of freezing his gonads off knee-deep in snow. Mist was a good excuse to give those gravestones a miss for a while. Last time he went up there he near enough caught a cold. It was impossible for him to catch colds, but still.

The Tudor's female counterpart appeared at his side, equally wide-eyed. "Who is this?" she said.

Something of an improvement, thought Divus, *usually they refer to me as an 'it.'*

"Yes," the man said. "Who are you?"

Divus hitched up his trousers and allowed himself an internal sigh. The little pleasures were those that made life worth living, or, if this weren't life, then whatever he was doing worth doing. "My name's Divus. I'm the caretaker of The End of Time."

"What, *you?*" the man said, unbelieving. "All alone?"

"Actually, my wife, Doris, works here too, so I don't get lonely, see?"

Doris popped out from behind a gravestone in the middle distance. "Someone say my name?"

This happened just about every meeting—it really got tedious after a while. These travellers always decided to approach him, never Doris. Maybe he had a wizened face, something like that. "No . . . yeah," Divus said. "I was just telling them who we are."

Doris rounded her gravestone and drew up to them. She gave them a grin. "You two lost, are you?"

"Yes," the man said, now doubly stunned by the pair of midgets confronting him—their pales faces and tangled blond hair no doubt reminding him of some kind of demon story he'd listened to on a dark and stormy night at some country estate.

The woman ducked out from beneath the man's armpit. "We'd be terribly appreciative if you'd tell us how to get back where we came from."

"And where'd you come from?" Divus said.

"Nineteen hundred and three."

Divus scratched his arse, getting his fingernails

right down into the crevice. "Dearie me, then what were you doing coming out of the Stone Age?"

The woman turned on the man. "I told you they weren't speaking French."

The man's eyes seemed to sink back into his skull. "Don't blame me, you're the one who's been abroad, remember?"

The couple bickered, back and forth, each blaming the other for their predicament.

This wasn't unusual either for Divus. Wanderers between different times often fell out with their companions. Being a mediator was somewhat outside his field of expertise, but he had to get them moving on somehow—otherwise he'd find himself beating off a migraine.

He held up his hands and shushed them. "Look, this isn't getting you anywhere. If you want to get back to where you've come from you two need to shut up and listen."

His brisk manner caught their attention. No matter the origin of the travellers, it usually did, after all he'd had a lot of practice.

"Now," Divus continued, "first things first. We've got to find the portal that's going to lead you back to your time."

The man set his hands on his hips and watched

Divus expectantly, as if he were some kind of customer service representative—that this whole mess was his fault by implication.

Divus wiped a layer of sweat from his forehead. "How did you get out of your time in the first place? You must've come through here at some point. How else would you have got to the Stone Age?"

"You tell me, midget," the man said. "You're clearly the expert."

Divus counted down from ten before continuing. "If you didn't come through here, then you must've stumbled through time, accidently found some rip in the space-time continuum, slipped right through it." He looked the couple over. "What were you doing when you were transported from your time?"

The man screwed up his features. "Really, midget—"

"Would you stop calling me that?" Divus said.

"Right, fine, little man."

Small victories, Divus thought. *Focus on the small victories.*

The man continued, "I don't see to what end it serves for us to tell you exactly the circumstances we were involved in when we were transported."

This pair might just be winning the award for the most ignorant and annoying of the day, if there had been days at The End of Time. Divus flashed his eyebrows, took to whistling a tune and moved off, headed for the next gravestone that needed attending to. Before he could leave the pair behind, however, Doris called out to him.

"Oi! Fatty. Where do you think you're going?"

Divus glanced back at her. "Had enough of these two. Maybe you can help them out."

Something about him being a 'grumpy old fart' drifted into Divus's hearing, his wife's appraisal of him. To be honest, Divus really didn't care. He just wanted to get on with his work. If the time travellers found their way back, good. If they managed to pick the touchstone leading to Inferno then all the better.

"Divus!" Doris said. "You come back here right now."

Divus took up his position at a fresh gravestone, an especially mucky one. He hocked up a great big wad of phlegm and let it loose. It splattered against the stone, running off in all directions. Before he even moved a muscle, he felt a tug at his belt. When he turned round he saw Doris there.

She squeezed her eyes together and pursed her lips. "If you don't come back and help these poor people right this moment then I'll go right off to Frank and tell him that you need reassigning to the

Hogs' Dimension, that you're not getting job satisfaction here."

Once, in the course of his scrubbing, Divus had come across the portal to the Hogs' Dimension, it had well and truly stunk of pig crap, and he had no intention of going there. He examined his wife and assessed whether or not she was bluffing. As always, her expression was plastered on, unreadable.

Divus shook his head. "Go tell him if you like. I'm filled up to here"—he indicated with his hand at his neck—"with these types drifting through, asking for directions and then giving out abuse when they don't like my response."

"They've been through a lot, dear."

"Yeah, well I've been through a lot putting up with their rubbish!"

"Don't shout, dear. You're making a scene."

Indeed, the Tudor couple were watching on, dewy-eyed, as Doris gave him the dressing down. Maybe, deep down, his wife was right—that these two people were good at heart and that circumstance had just played tricks on them, turned them bitter.

She laid her hand on his forearm. "You know this place better than anyone. If anyone can help them out, find their way back home, it's you."

Although Divus knew that was somewhat faint praise, given Doris knew The End of Time just as well as he did, if not better. But he appreciated the sentiment, the effort she was making to make him feel valued. Perhaps, after he helped these two, they could speak to Frank, maybe negotiate some holiday. If there was one thing that played into an employer's hands at The End of Time it was that, with no stringent measure of time, they could take liberties with employee working hours.

"What do you say?" Doris said.

Divus glanced back over the Tudor couple again. They did look particularly pathetic, completely hopeless. He gave his wife a peck on the forehead and strode over to them, managing a faint smile as he went. "If I'm going to help you folks you've got to be honest with me, tell me what happened to get you here."

The man and woman exchanged glances, then the man looked into Divus's eyes. "We were at my Auntie Margaret's, a Christmas party."

"There," Divus said, "that wasn't so hard now, was it?"

The man fidgeted with his hands. "Yes, well, you see, Lindsay here is my brother's wife, and, you know how things are, we were fooling around in the guest bedroom when we heard someone coming, decided to hide in a cupboard. And that's when we got thrown into another world."

Divus never would work out these humans' propensity for embarrassment, how they somehow twisted every situation round, made it as awkward for everyone involved as possible. He wondered if they did it on purpose. "You got sent to the Stone Age?" Divus said.

"Yes," the man said.

The woman butted in. "We didn't break anything, I promise."

These humans were always so full of self-importance, they thought that they had some unwieldy power to affect a lasting change in the world. Had they not looked round them? Seen that all of their kind were marked with gravestones? Now wasn't the time for arguments though, he needed to get these people back quickly and efficiently.

"This way," Divus said, leading them through the gravestones, already working out—with the map in his brain—exactly where their best point of entry might be. As they wandered on, he turned back to them and said, "So how did you manage to get out of the Stone Age?"

"Oh," the man said, "we found a mystical forest. All we had to do was touch a knot on a tree and we got sent back here."

The woman nudged him in the ribs.

"Ouch!" the man said. "Well, in truth there was

another man there, he was wearing a very strange suit, some sort of odd underwear."

As Divus's eyes darted over the inscriptions in the stones, trying to locate where they needed to go, he said, "Yes, he'll be a straggler from the thirty-sixth century. They went through a period of time travel. Got bored of it, though, after a while. Just like the rest of us."

The man's lips flapped open. "You mean to say that someone, somewhere, has invented time travel."

Divus sneered, approaching the appropriate stone. He rested his elbow against it and turned back to them. "You don't 'invent' time travel, you discover it. And you'll be unsurprised to hear that your mediocre race was one of the slowest on record to do that, or so Frank says."

"Who's Frank?" the woman said, scowling, perhaps slighted by his blunt assessment of humankind.

"He's the Master of Time," Divus said.

"Oh," she said.

"For you lot, anyway." Divus patted the gravestone then stepped away from it. "This is your way back."

The man stooped to read the inscription. "Walter P Ebberson." He straightened up. "Who's that?"

Divus shrugged. "Dunno, some other human.

Nothing special about him. He just happened to die round the time you're looking for."

The man glanced round. "So this is it? I just touch the stone here and we go back."

"Yes," Divus said, getting impatient.

The man looked to his companion and smiled. He turned back to Divus. "You know, all this time travelling has been rather marvellous, and, actually, it might be something of an adventure were we to—"

Divus lurched forward and snatched both of them by the wrist. He yanked them forward and held them against the cold stone. Being a time demon himself, he had no need to worry about the teleportation powers of the stone. He could quite easily slip between dimensions and worlds without the aid of training wheels.

The man and woman turned into bright white silhouettes, their arms flailing, not quite wanting to go back to their own time.

As he walked away from the tombstone, he hoped against hope that they wouldn't work out how to get back here. It really was half the story if they managed to work out that there was more to Rutsley Church and Burial Grounds than met the eye. Divus looked across the graveyard, to the dilapidated church, mere ruins now.

As he whipped out his cloth, got ready to polish

up another stone, he overheard his wife calling out to him.

"Divus! Divus! Got a man here. He's lost."

Divus didn't even bother to gob on the tombstone. He might as well re-label himself as Official Tour Guide of The End of Time. He wondered if that job might offer better hours. Perhaps later on, when he got a spare minute, he would ask Frank.

AUTHOR'S NOTE

Thank you for taking the time to read one of my books. If you would like to hear about my latest releases you can sign up for my newsletter here: www.raymondsflex.com

Thanks for reading!

Raymond S Flex

Stories From The World Of Ethereal